Tomochichi
Chief and Friend

Heather E. Schwartz

Consultants

Regina Holland, Ed.S., *Henry County Schools;* **Christina Noblet, Ed.S.**, *Paulding County; School District;* **Jennifer Troyer**, *Paulding County Schools;* **David Proctor**, *Muscogee (Creek) Cultural Advisor;* **John Ross**, *Certified Cherokee Language Teacher;* **Karen Coody Cooper, M.A.**, *Cherokee Historian*

Publishing Credits

Rachelle Cracchiolo, M.S.Ed., *Publisher*
Conni Medina, M.A.Ed., *Managing Editor*
Emily R. Smith, M.A.Ed., *Series Developer*
Diana Kenney, M.A.Ed., NBCT, *Content Director*
Torrey Maloof, *Editor*
Courtney Patterson, *Multimedia Designer*

Image Credits: pp. 25, 29, 32 Alamy; p. 5 Blue Lantern Studio/Corbis; pp. 2, 26, 29 Ken Lund/Flickr; p. 17 Jennifer Broadus/Getty Images; pp. 21, 23 back cover (background) iStock; pp. 2, 10 LOC [LC-USZ62-48951]; p. 16 Ed Jackson; pp. front cover, 1–3, 6–7, 9, 19–20, 22, 31 North Wind Pictures; pp. 3–4, 11, 18, 24, 27, 29 Wikimedia Commons; pp. 13–15 Timothy J. Bradley; All other images from iStock and/or Shutterstock.

Library of Congress Cataloging-in-Publication Data

Names: Schwartz, Heather E., author.
Title: Tomochichi : chief and friend / Heather Schwartz.
Description: Huntington Beach, CA : Teacher Created Materials, [2016] |
Includes index. | Audience: Grades K to 3.?
Identifiers: LCCN 2015042468 | ISBN 9781493825561 (pbk.)
Subjects: LCSH: Tomo-chi-chi, -1739--Juvenile literature. | Yamassee
Indians--Biography--Juvenile literature. | Yamassee
Indians--History--Juvenile literature. | Georgia--History--Colonial
period, ca. 1600-1775--Juvenile literature. | Oglethorpe, James,
1696-1785--Juvenile literature.
Classification: LCC E99.Y22 S38 2016 | DDC 975.004/973850092--dc23
LC record available at http://lccn.loc.gov/2015042468

Teacher Created Materials
5301 Oceanus Drive
Huntington Beach, CA 92649-1030
http://www.tcmpub.com
ISBN 978-1-4938-2556-1

Table of Contents

War or Peace?

In 1733, a group of British **settlers** came to the New World. They wanted a better life. They planned to start a new **colony** (KAHL-uh-nee). It would be called Georgia.

When the settlers arrived, there were American Indians already living on the land. The settlers did not know what would happen next. Could they find good land to grow crops? Would the **tribes** give them furs and leather? Would there be peace or war? **Chief** Tomochichi played a key role in answering these questions. This is his story.

Tomochichi

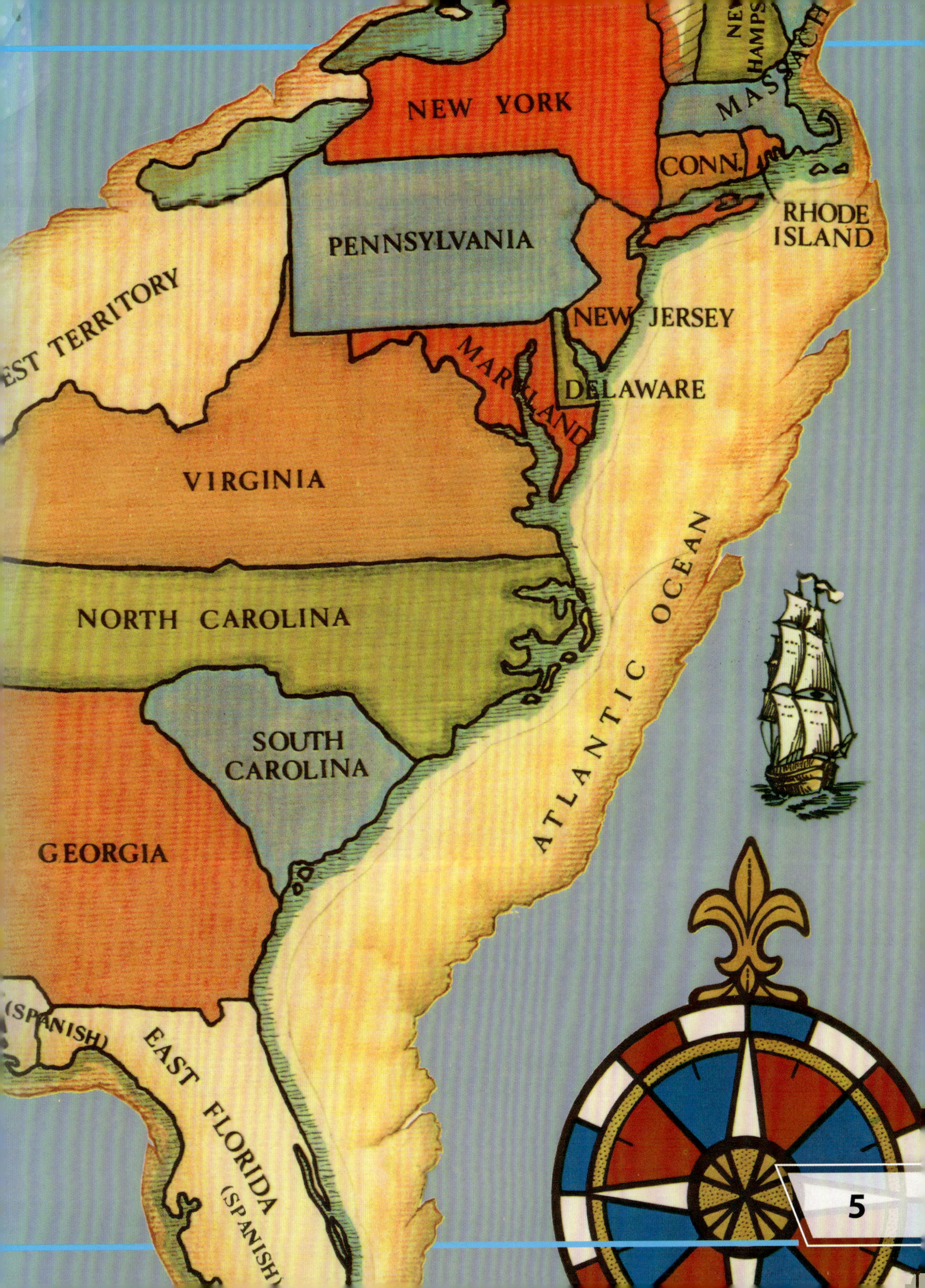
NEW YORK
NEW HAMPS
MASSACH
CONN.
RHODE ISLAND
PENNSYLVANIA
EST TERRITORY
NEW JERSEY
MARYLAND
DELAWARE
VIRGINIA
NORTH CAROLINA
SOUTH CAROLINA
GEORGIA
ATLANTIC OCEAN
(SPANISH)
EAST FLORIDA (SPANISH)

Early Peacemaker

We don't know much about Tomochichi when he was young. We do know he grew up to be a chief. A chief is a leader. He must have been brave and strong. He was probably a good warrior and hunter, too!

Older and Wiser

Tomochichi was not a young man when the settlers arrived. He was already in his late 80s.

In 1728, there were two tribes. One was the Creek. The other was the Yamasee (YAH-muh-see). The two tribes were fighting. They disagreed about the settlers. They didn't know what to do about them. Tomochichi had a plan.

Tomochichi was going to help the settlers. But he would also be cautious. In the past, white settlers had not always been honest or kind to his people.

He decided to make a new tribe. He would be the chief. He took people from the Creek and the Yamasee tribes. The new tribe was called the Yamacraw (YAH-muh-kraw). They liked his ideas about the settlers. They found a new place to live on the bluffs of the Savannah River.

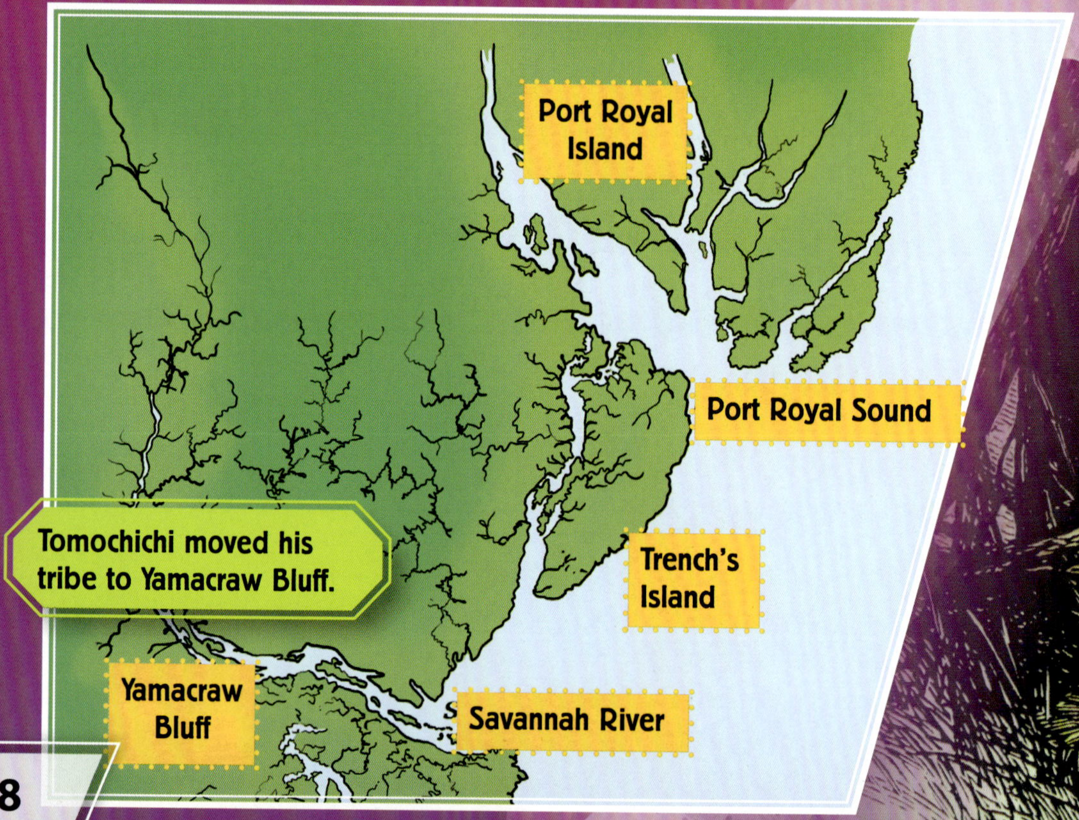

Why the Bluffs?

Tomochichi chose the bluffs because they were the burial ground of his relatives. They were also near a trading post. Trading posts were places people went to trade for things that they needed.

Settling the Land

At the same time, a man named James Oglethorpe made plans. He wanted to sail from Great Britain to the New World. He wanted to start a new colony.

Name Game

James chose the name Georgia in honor of the king of Great Britain, George II.

Years later, James left Great Britain. About 114 settlers went with him. There were men, women, and children. They crossed the Atlantic Ocean on a ship called the *Anne*. The trip took two months. In 1733, they arrived in the New World.

James wanted to settle near the Savannah River. He would call his new town Savannah. But the Yamacraw were living there. James did not want to start trouble. He wanted to get permission from the tribe. He wanted to share the land.

To share his plan, James wanted to speak with the chief. But he did not know how. He did not know their language. And Tomochichi did not speak English. Luckily, there was a special woman. She spoke both languages! Her name was Mary Musgrove. She helped the two men talk to each other.

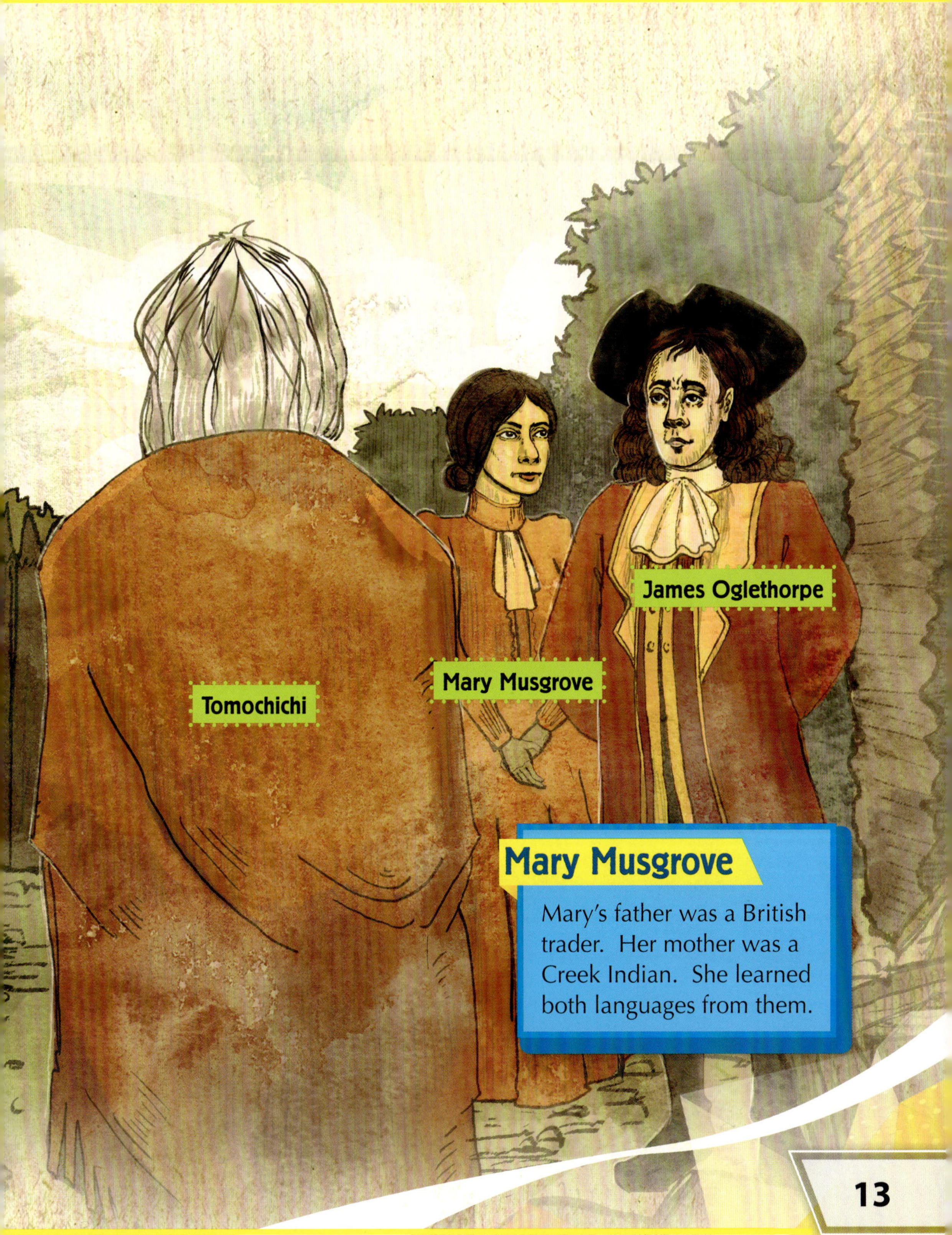

Mary Musgrove

Mary's father was a British trader. Her mother was a Creek Indian. She learned both languages from them.

The two men made a deal. They signed a **treaty**. They were going to share the land. The two groups would also trade goods. The Yamacraw gave the settlers deer and buffalo skins. The settlers gave the Yamacraw cloth, metal tools, and guns.

There was one other thing Tomochichi asked for. He asked the settlers to teach his tribe about being **Christian** (KRIS-chuhn). He thought this would make the friendship stronger between the two groups.

Friendship Gift

Tomochichi gave James a deerskin as a gift. It had symbols that stood for their new friendship.

Working Together

James and Tomochichi treated each other with respect. They were good role models for their groups. The Yamacraw and the British came from very different **cultures**. Yet the two groups got along. They had good leaders to help them. They learned from each other. They worked hard together. They helped each other when they could.

Tomochichi shared his own land. He let the settlers use the land near his home. He also helped them build roads. He even helped build the very first road out of Savannah. This road went to the town of New Inverness. Today, that town is called Darien.

This is what an artist thought Tomochichi, Mary, and James looked like.

This is Darien today.

James respected the Yamacraw way of life. He honored their **customs** and **rights**. He kept the promises he made to them. He protected them. He told them which traders should not be trusted. James did not want them to be taken advantage of.

In 1734, James took a trip. He traveled back to Great Britain. But he brought a special guest with him. He brought Tomochichi! The chief traveled with other men from his tribe. Tomochichi brought his wife and his nephew, too.

Tomochichi goes to a meeting in Great Britain.

Next In Line

Toonahowi was Tomochichi's nephew. Tomochichi treated him like a son. Toonahowi was next in line to become chief.

This is Kensington Palace where Tomochichi met with King George II.

Tomochichi hoped to meet with leaders in Great Britain. He had two goals for his trip. He wanted to protect his people. And he wanted to keep peace between his people and the British settlers.

The chief met with many leaders on his visit. He spoke well. People listened to his ideas. Then, he met the king! They talked about fair trade. The chief did not want his people to be cheated out of a good trade. They also talked about **religion**. The chief said he wanted his people to learn about being Christian. He wanted schools for his people.

A Special Gift

Tomochichi brought King George II a special gift. He gave the king eagle feathers as a token of peace.

Peaceful Times

Tomochichi's travels to Great Britain lasted six months. Then, he returned home to Georgia. He met with other chiefs. He told them about his trip. He said that the British were honest. He told the chiefs they could trust the British.

A few months later, Tomochichi got great news. The British were going to build a school. It would be for the children of the local tribes. It would be a Christian school. In 1736, the school opened. Tomochichi was pleased. This was his proof the British wanted peace. They wanted a friendship with his people.

The schoolhouse that the British built may have looked like this one.

Students studied the Bible in school.

Tomochichi's Legacy

Tomochichi and James stayed close friends. James would often ask the chief for advice. The chief was glad to help James when he could.

In 1739, Tomochichi was quite old. He became ill and died that same year. Before his death, he asked to be buried in Savannah. He wanted to be close to his people and his British friends. James was at his funeral. He wished to honor his dear friend. He had a pyramid of stones placed on the chief's grave. This was an American Indian tradition.

In Honor Of

Later, a large rock was placed on Tomochichi's grave. It has a bronze **plaque** (PLAK) on it. The words on the plaque honor Tomochichi.

Tomochichi was a strong leader. He was a loyal friend. He wanted peace, not war. And he worked hard to keep that peace. He knew how to use his power wisely. He knew his words would go a long way.

The great chief played an important role in creating the town of Savannah. And he took care of his own people along the way. He helped make the state of Georgia what it is today.

The Tomochichi Federal Building and U.S. Courthouse was named in honor of the chief in 2005.

Build It!

A monument honors a special person or an event. Think about what you read in this book. What made Tomochichi unique (yoo-NEEK)? Design a monument to honor the great chief. Build it with clay or construction paper.

GEORGIA
1776
TOMO-CHI-CHI'S GRAVE
Tomo-Chi-Chi, Mico of the Yamacraws, a tribe of the Creek Indian Nation, is buried in this Square. He has been called a co-founder, with Oglethorpe, of Georgia. He was a good friend to the English, a friendship indispensable to the establishment of the Colony as a military outpost against Spanish invasion. He negotiated with Oglethorpe the treaty, formally ratified on May 21, 1733, pursuant to which Georgia was settled. Mary Musgrove, half-breed niece of Emperor Brim of the Creek Indians, acted as interpreter between Oglethorpe and Tomo-Chi-Chi and lent her great influence to the signing of that treaty and to the treaties negotiated by Oglethorpe with other tribes of the Creek nation.

Glossary

chief—the person who is the leader of a group of people

Christian—a person who believes in the teachings of Jesus Christ

colony—an area ruled by a faraway country

cultures—the beliefs and ways of groups of people

customs—traditional behaviors or actions of a group of people

plaque—a flat, thin piece of metal or wood with writing on it that is used as a reminder of something

religion—a system of beliefs and rules

rights—things that a person is allowed to have and do

settlers—people who go to live in a new place where there are few other people

treaty—a deal that is made between two or more countries or groups

tribes—groups of people that have the same language, customs, and beliefs

Index

Your Turn!

Important Words

The rock that was placed on Tomochichi's grave has a plaque. It gives details about his life. What details would you want people to know about you? Brainstorm and design a plaque for your life.